To:

From:

The days slowly pass,
and the nights are long.
Linus the Wizard
decides to go home.

I'll grab my hat,
I'll grab my wand,
then journey home,
to rest in my pond!

As Linus hopped
by the lake,
He was met by Steele
the Snake.

"Head up North.
That's what you should do.
I have many friends for you."

I'll grab my hat,
I'll grab my wand,
then journey home,
to rest in my pond!

As Linus hopped
by the big oak tree,
He was met by Burt
the Bee.

"Going East would be better.
Because the East
has the best weather."

I'll grab my hat,
I'll grab my wand,
then journey home,
to rest in my pond!

As Linus hopped
by the big dirt mound,
He was met by Baxter
the Hound.

"Head out West
for a beautiful hike.
The West has delicious
bugs you like."

I'll grab my hat,
I'll grab my wand,
then journey home,
to rest in my pond!

As Linus hopped by a hole,
He was met by Misty
the Mole.

"In the South,
there's not much fog.
Plus you'll find
so many frogs!"

I'll grab my hat,
I'll grab my wand,
then journey home,
to rest in my pond!

There are always places to go,
and people to see,
but home is home,
and that's where I'll be!

The End.

First edition August 2020

ISBN 978-1-7355971-2-6 (hardback)
ISBN 978-1-7355971-1-9 (paperback)
ISBN 978-1-7355971-0-2 (ebook)

www.linusthewizard.com